Puppy Princess

Wish Upon a Star

Puppy Princess

Wish Upon a Star

by Patty Furlington

Scholastic Inc.

With special thanks to Anne Marie Ryan

ISBN 978-1-338-13432-2

10 9 8 7 6 5 4 3 2 1 18 19 20 21 22

Printed in the U.S.A. 40
First printing 2018

Book design by Baily Crawford

Table of Contents

Petrovia Royal Family
Rosie
Queen Fifi
King Charles
Rocky & Rollo

Chapter 1

An Exciting Announcement

"Don't call me mild, because I'm really wild," a white puppy with curly hair sang at the top of her lungs. In her paws, she clutched a bone as if it was a microphone.

"If you don't like my roar, then I'll show you the door," a fluffy gray kitten meowed into her own bone microphone.

The puppy and kitten belted out the final

chorus together. *"So come on and get down with the coolest cat in town!"*

"I love Bella Fierce sooooo much," said Rosie, the puppy.

"She's amazing," said Cleo, the kitten, gazing at the posters of Bella Fierce plastered all over Rosie's bedroom walls.

Bella Fierce was the biggest pop star in Petrovia. A sleek Siamese cat with one blue eye and one brown eye, Bella Fierce strutted like an alley cat and sang her hits in a throaty purr. Rosie and her best friend, Cleo, were huge fans and knew the words to all of her songs by heart.

The posters looked slightly out of place in Rosie's elegant bedroom. Windows draped by velvet curtains looked out onto sprawling gardens. There was an enormous four-poster bed with a pink satin bedspread decorated with the royal paw print. On the bedside table, a diamond tiara dangled from a reading lamp, and jeweled collars spilled out of the drawer.

This wasn't an ordinary puppy's bedroom, because Rosie wasn't an ordinary puppy—she was Princess Rosie, heir to the throne of Petrovia! Cleo wasn't just her best friend, either; the kitten was also her lady-in-waiting. She helped with Rosie's royal duties, but the two mostly played and had fun together.

A white puppy with floppy ears and curly hair just like Rosie's burst into the bedroom, his tail wagging. "What's wrong?" Prince Rocky asked.

Another puppy, identical to Rocky except for a black splodge over one eye, bounded into the room behind his brother. "Is some-one hurt?" Prince Rollo said.

Rosie and Cleo exchanged puzzled looks.

Rosie shook her head, her ears flapping. "Nobody's hurt," she told her brothers.

"Then why were you two howling?" Rocky asked.

"We weren't howling," Cleo said. "We were singing!"

"Oops!" said Rollo. "Easy mistake to make." The two princes rolled on the floor, giggling.

"Ha-ha," said Rosie sarcastically, throwing her bone microphone at Rocky. "You two are hilarious."

That just made the princes laugh even harder.

Rosie grabbed Cleo's bone and chucked it at Rollo, but instead of hitting the prince, it hit a gray bunny in a white apron who had just hopped into Rosie's bedroom. The bone knocked the bunny's starched white cap onto the floor.

"Sorry, Priscilla!" said Rosie. "I wasn't trying to hit you. I was trying to hit Rollo."

"Huff!" said Priscilla. "A princess should NEVER throw things."

Rosie rolled her chocolate-brown eyes. She was so glad that prim and proper Priscilla was no longer her lady-in-waiting! Fed up with the bunny's rules and regulations, Rosie had sneaked out of the palace and met Cleo, sharing a wonderful adventure with her. From that day on, Cleo had been her lady-in-waiting, and Priscilla had been promoted to Pawstone Palace's chief housekeeper. Everyone was much happier that way!

"Did you think they were howling in pain?" Rocky asked Priscilla playfully.

"Certainly not!" said Priscilla. "I came to remind Princess Rosie that Bruno has arrived for her dance lesson. He is waiting in the ballroom." Sniffing, she picked up her cap, put it back on her head, and hopped out of the room.

Rosie groaned loudly. "Ugh! I hate dance lessons!"

"Why?" asked Cleo. "Dancing is fun."

"Not when Bruno's your teacher," muttered Rosie. "He makes me do boring ballroom dancing."

Rosie and Cleo went downstairs to the ballroom. Outside the gold doors, carved with figures of dancing animals, Rosie and Cleo hugged good-bye.

"See you tomorrow," Cleo said.

Inside the ballroom, a small sausage dog with a gleaming brown coat tapped his paw impatiently. "You're late, Princess Rosie!" snapped Bruno. "But then, I already knew that you have no sense of timing."

Priscilla, who was hopping around the ballroom with a feather duster, giggled.

Rosie sighed. She hadn't even started

dancing yet and the lesson was already going badly!

"We'll start with the waltz. Remember," said Bruno, turning on the music and gliding around the room to demonstrate, "you must use long, smooth, flowing movements."

He took Rosie's paws, and they began to dance around the room.

"One, two, three," Bruno counted the beat aloud. "One, two—" Bruno stopped and waved his paws in the air. "No! No! No!" he cried. "In the waltz your paws must glide, not stomp!"

"Sorry, Bruno," Rosie said, her tail between her legs.

"Let's take it from the top," said Bruno, starting the music again.

This time, Rosie tried to make her paws glide gracefully across the polished wooden floor. *One, two, three,* she counted in her head. *One, two, threeeeeeeeee*– Rosie slipped and fell on the floor, pulling Bruno down with her.

Priscilla hopped over and helped them up.

Brushing his hair off, Bruno said, "That's enough waltzing for one day."

"Can we dance to something by Bella Fierce?" Rosie asked her teacher eagerly.

"Huff! Huffity-huff!" Priscilla tutted loudly, looking up from her dusting.

Bruno shook his head disapprovingly. "Absolutely not!" he said. "Queen Fifi has hired me to teach you ballroom dancing, not how to wiggle like a pop star!" Holding out his paws to Rosie, Bruno said, "We'll do the cha-cha next."

Oh no, thought Rosie. The cha-cha had fast, tricky footwork.

"One, two, cha-cha-cha," counted Bruno as they danced around the room.

Rosie desperately tried to move her paws and shake her tail in time with the music.

"One, two, cha-cha-OW!" wailed Bruno as Rosie accidentally stepped on his paw.

"I'm so sorry!" said Rosie.

"We'll stop there!" barked Bruno, limping away from Rosie. "I can't risk injuring another paw."

"Let's get you some ice," said Priscilla, helping Bruno hobble out of the ballroom.

Rosie's eyes filled with tears. She felt like she had four left paws!

Later that evening, Rosie ate dinner in the formal dining room with the rest of the royal family.

"Mmm, this stew is delicious," said Rosie's father, King Charles, licking his chops. The tubby white Maltese had already eaten two helpings.

Petal, the palace's guinea pig cook, *did* make very tasty stew. But Rosie didn't have much of an appetite tonight.

"You're very quiet, Rosie," said Queen

Fifi, a perfectly groomed white Maltese wearing a diamond collar. "How was your dance lesson?"

"Awful," whimpered Rosie, hiding her face in her paw. "I stepped on Bruno's paw."

"You just need more practice," said King Charles kindly. "I'm sure you're not as bad as you think you are."

"Have you seen Rosie dance?" said Rocky.

"Her dancing's almost as good as her singing," said Rollo, giggling.

"I hate dance lessons," whined Rosie. "I wish I could quit!"

"No," her mother said firmly. "When you are queen of Petrovia, you will attend lots of balls. It's important that you know how to dance."

"When I'm the queen, *I'll* get to make the rules," Rosie grumbled. "The first thing I'll do is ban ballroom dancing."

"We'll see," said Queen Fifi, sounding unconcerned.

"I've got some news that might cheer you up," said King Charles.

Rosie's ears perked up.

"It's time for the Royal Talent Show!" announced the king.

Rosie and her brothers yelped with excitement. Every winter there was a talent show in Petrovia, and it was always lots of fun!

King Charles hadn't finished. "Rosie," he said, "we think that you are ready to take on more responsibility."

Queen Fifi smiled at her daughter. "This year we'd like you to organize the talent show!"

Chapter 2

Snow Day

"Rosie, Rosie! Wake up!" cried Prince Rollo, leaping on the bed and licking his sister's face.

"Let me sleep," groaned Rosie, hiding her head under a pillow. She was having a wonderful dream that she and Cleo were at a Bella Fierce concert singing along to all the songs.

Prince Rocky bit the corner of Rosie's bedspread and dragged it off her bed.

"Hey!" Rosie yelped, scrabbling with her paws to try to get it back. "It's cold."

"Duh!" said Rollo. "We know it's cold. In fact, it's so cold that it—"

"SNOWED!" cried Rocky.

Now Rosie was wide awake! She jumped out of bed and bounded to the window. Resting her paws on the sill, she pressed her damp black nose against the glass. The grounds of Pawstone Palace were covered in a sparkling blanket of white snow!

"Yay!" she cried. "We can build snow dogs!"

"And have a snowball fight!" said Rocky, joining her at the window.

"What's that?" asked Rollo, pointing his paw at something pink in the distance.

"It's Cleo!" laughed Rosie. The gray kitten was making her way to the palace. Only her pink collar stood out against the snowdrifts!

"I can't wait to tell Cleo about the talent show!" said Rosie, her tail wagging. Rosie suddenly realized that there would be no time for snow dogs and snowball fights. She had important work to do!

Quickly putting on her ruby collar, Rosie yanked a brush through her curly fur.

"I can't believe we didn't win last year," grumbled Rocky.

"Yeah, we were robbed," said Rollo. "We should have won first prize."

Last year the princes had entered the talent show as a comedy double act. Their imitation of their parents had been a huge hit with everyone in the audience except for Queen Fifi, who felt that it hadn't shown proper respect.

"What do you call a snow dog in the summer?" Rocky asked Rosie.

"I don't know," she said. "What?"

"A puddle!" cried Rollo, howling with laughter.

Rosie groaned.

"Wait! I've got another one," said Rocky. "What do snow dogs eat for lunch?"

"Ice burgers!" shrieked Rollo. The twins rolled on their backs, waving their paws in the air as they yelped with laughter.

"Yes, it's astonishing that you didn't win," said Rosie, rolling her eyes. "Now, if you'll excuse me, some of us have work to do," she said, feeling very important.

Rosie headed downstairs to greet Cleo.

"Ah, Rosie," said the king, coming out of the dining room with crumbs on his whiskers. He was with Theodore, an ancient tortoise who had been the royal family's butler for several generations. "I was just coming to find you. Could you start spreading the news about the talent show around Petrovia today?"

"No problem!" said Rosie. Proud to have been entrusted with such a big responsibility, Rosie couldn't wait to get started!

Very, very slowly, Theodore handed Rosie a stack of posters announcing the talent show. Rosie could see why King Charles didn't want the old tortoise to deliver them—it would take Theodore years to crawl around Petrovia!

"Hi, Rosie," said Cleo, coming into the palace and stamping her paws to warm them up. Her blue eyes sparkled, and her nose was even pinker than usual. "Are you excited about the snow?"

"Yes," said Rosie. "But I'm even more excited about the Royal Talent Show!"

Cleo gasped. "Is it happening soon?"

"Really soon," said Rosie. "And this year my parents have asked me to organize it!"

"Wow!" said Cleo, impressed. "Do you need some help?"

"My first job is hanging these up around Petrovia," explained Rosie, showing Cleo the posters. "Want to come with me?"

"Of course," purred Cleo.

Rosie and Cleo set off as soon as Rosie had eaten breakfast. They ran into the frosty air, each carrying a big stack of posters in a sack.

"Brrr!" said Rosie, shivering.

"You'll warm up if we run," said Cleo, her paws sinking into the snow as she dashed ahead.

Giggling, Rosie chased after her friend. Her breath puffed out like smoke as she bounded through the powdery snow.

POW! POW! POW! Snowballs pelted Rosie and Cleo. One hit Rosie right on her head! *SPLAT!*

"Hey!" she cried, shaking snow off her fur. "Where did those come from?"

There was no sign of their attackers. Rosie's eyes could only see pure white snow. Her ears, however, heard giggling coming from behind a snow-covered holly bush. "Do you hear that?" she whispered to Cleo.

Cleo nodded. The girls each formed a snowball, and they crept stealthily toward the bush.

"Gotcha!" Rosie shouted, jumping behind the bush. She hurled her snowball and hit Rocky on the back.

"Take that!" cried Cleo, firing her

snowball. Rollo spun around in alarm, and the snowball hit him right on the nose. *SMACK!*

"Bull's-eye!" Rosie shouted triumphantly.

Scooping up snow, the princes threw more snowballs at the girls. Rosie and Cleo fought back, launching their own snowballs

at Rocky and Rollo. The crisp winter air rang with shouts and laughter as snowballs flew through the sky.

"Time-out!" yelled Rosie, panting. Everyone stopped throwing snowballs and caught their breath. "Cleo and I need to go deliver posters for the talent show."

"That reminds me—Rocky and I need to go rehearse our act," said Rollo, brushing snow off his paws.

"What kind of act are you doing?" Cleo asked.

"It's a secret," Rocky said mysteriously.

"But it's going to be amazing," said Rollo.

Heading toward the palace gates, Rosie and Cleo met a squirrel with a bushy gray tail shoveling snow. Big white snowbanks were piled up on either side of the path he'd cleared.

"Good morning, Hamish!" Rosie called to the palace's head gardener.

"Good morning, Your Highness," Hamish replied, taking off his woolly cap and bowing. "Have you come outside to play in the snow?"

"We don't have time to play," said Rosie. "We've got an important job to do." She showed Hamish one of the posters. "We need to hang these up all over the kingdom."

Hamish chuckled and said, "I'll dust off my bagpipes and start practicing."

"We'd better be on our way," said Rosie.

"There's a sled in the garden shed that belonged to King Charles when he was a boy," said Hamish. "It might help you get around faster."

"Great idea! Thanks, Hamish!" Rosie said. She and Cleo trudged through the snow to the shed. Propped at the back, behind a wheelbarrow, was an old wooden sled with shiny red metal runners. They dragged it to the top of a slope and sat on it—Rosie at the front, and Cleo at the back, her paws wrapped around Rosie's middle.

"WHEE!" Rosie and Cleo shot across the snow. The cold wind blew Rosie's ears back as the sled picked up speed and flew down the hillside. "YIPPEEE!" Rosie yipped for joy.

In no time at all, they arrived in the village of Oak Tree Hollow. As Rosie hung one of the posters on the trunk of a big oak tree, their squirrel friend, Charlie, came out of a cozy house shaped like an acorn.

"Hi, Princess Rosie! Hi, Cleo," he greeted them. "Whatcha doin'?"

"We're letting everyone know about the Royal Talent Show," Rosie told him.

"Ooh!" Charlie said, twitching his bushy tail. "I'm going to enter this year!"

"What's your talent?" Cleo asked him.

"Juggling!" Charlie said. He dashed back into his house and came out again holding three acorns. "Watch!"

Charlie threw the acorns into the air. He

caught one, but missed the other two nuts. One fell into the snow, and the other bonked Rosie on the head!

"Oops!" said Charlie. "Sorry, Princess Rosie. I guess I need more practice!"

"Good luck," Rosie told him, rubbing her head. Then Cleo climbed onto the sled and Rosie pulled her along to the next village.

Taking turns riding on the sled, the girls traveled far and wide, hanging up posters in every corner of Petrovia. Lots of animals they met told them that they were going to enter the talent show.

By the time they arrived in Hamster Hamlet, the girls were feeling cold and tired.

"You look like you could use a warm drink," their friend Elsie said.

The little hamster invited them into her burrow for a cup of blackberry tea.

"This is just what I needed," Rosie said happily, warming her paws on the cup and inhaling the fruity scent.

"Are you going to enter the talent show, Elsie?" Cleo asked.

"I'm not very talented," Elsie said.

"There must be something you could do," Rosie said.

Elsie thought for a moment. "There *is* one trick I can do," she told them. Elsie crammed ten plump berries into her bulging cheeks.

"That's very . . . er . . . unique," Rosie told her politely.

After finishing their drinks, the girls went back out into the cold. The sky had turned a beautiful shade of pink as the sun began to set.

"I had no idea there was so much talent in Petrovia," Rosie said cheerfully. "This is going to be the best talent show ever!"

"Yes," said Cleo softly, though she didn't sound very happy about it.

"I'd better hurry home before it gets dark," Rosie said. "Want to have dinner at the palace?"

"No, thanks," said Cleo, shaking her head sadly. "I'll just head back to Catnip Corner."

"Would you mind hanging up a few posters while you're there?" Rosie asked her.

Cleo nodded, then trudged off in the direction of her village.

"See you soon," Rosie called out to her friend, but she didn't get a reply.

Cleo's acting weird, she thought to herself as she pulled the sled back to the palace. *She's probably just cold and tired.*

Rocky and Rollo pounced on Rosie the second she returned home.

"Rosie's back!" cried Rocky.

"Tell us now, Dad!" said Rollo.

"What's going on?" asked Rosie. Melting snow dripped off her fur, leaving a puddle on the floor.

"I have more exciting news, but wanted to wait until you got back," said King Charles, smiling at the three puppies. "This year's talent show is going to be judged by . . . Bella Fierce!"

Chapter 3

Cleo's Secret

The next morning, Rosie didn't need an alarm clock or even her brothers to wake her up. She jumped out of bed at the crack of dawn, eager to start work. Rosie really wanted to prove that her parents were right to trust her with such an important job!

Glancing up at a poster of Bella singing into a microphone, Rosie shivered with excitement. She couldn't believe her idol was actually coming to visit!

The palace was silent except for the sound of Rosie's rumbling tummy. Rosie padded softly downstairs, not wanting to wake anyone up. The dining room table wasn't set for breakfast yet, so she headed to the kitchen to grab a quick bite.

The kitchen was in the basement, and as Rosie trotted down the stairs, her ears perked up. Someone was singing!

Petal, the palace's chef, was wearing headphones and singing opera loudly as she stirred a big pot of oatmeal on the stove.

"Morning, Petal," said Rosie, but the guinea pig didn't hear her.

"Tra la la la!" sang Petal.

"Hi, Petal," Rosie tried again, a bit louder.

"La la ti daaaa . . ." Petal trilled. The glasses in the kitchen cabinets started to rattle dangerously as she hit a very high note.

"Ahem!" Rosie coughed loudly.

"Oh!" squealed Petal, jumping and dropping her spoon with a clatter. Taking off her headphones, she said, "Your Highness! You scared the living daylights out of me!"

"Sorry, Petal," said Rosie, picking up the spoon. "I didn't mean to frighten you."

"I hope my singing didn't wake you up," said Petal.

"No," Rosie assured her. "I got up early because I've got a lot to do today. I'm organizing the Royal Talent Show," she told the cook proudly.

"That's wonderful!" said Petal. "That's why I was practicing. I'm going to sing opera in the show."

"Cool," said Rosie. "Have you heard who the judge is going to be?"

Petal got a clean spoon out of a drawer and returned to stirring the oatmeal. "Who?" she asked.

"Bella Fierce!" Rosie announced.

"Oh my!" Petal gasped, nearly dropping the spoon again. "I adore her!"

Rosie winced as Petal started singing one of Bella Fierce's songs in the style of an opera singer. It was all she could do not to cover her ears with her paws!

"Well, I'd better get to work," she told Petal.

"Don't you want some oatmeal?" Petal asked, waving the spoon like a conductor's baton.

"No, thanks," said Rosie, grabbing a freshly baked muffin. "I'll have one of these."

Munching the delicious banana-nut muffin, Rosie hurried out of the kitchen. She liked Petal's baking a lot more than her singing!

Right, Rosie said to herself, *first I need to find Theodore.* The butler was usually up bright and early. Rosie searched for Theodore in the throne room, the dining room, and the ballroom, but there was no sign of him anywhere. *Hmm, where could he be?* she thought.

Rosie peeked in the parlor, but Theodore wasn't in there, either. Instead, six bunny maids were standing on top of one another to make a pyramid.

Shaking their feather dusters like cheerleaders' pom-poms, the maids cried, "Give me a P-E-T-R-O-V-I-A!"

"Petrovia!" Rosie called out.

Startled, the bunny at the top of the

pyramid started to wobble. WHOOPS! The pyramid collapsed, and the bunnies fell on their fluffy tails.

Rosie rushed over and helped them up.

"Sorry, Princess Rosie," said one of the maids, straightening her apron. "We were rehearsing our cheerleading routine for the Royal Talent Show."

"It's looking good," said Rosie. "Have you seen Theodore?"

None of the cheerleading maids had seen the butler.

Rosie headed back upstairs. The rest of her family would be awake by now—perhaps Theodore was with them.

"Hi, Mom," she said, spotting Queen Fifi emerging from her royal bedchamber and stretching her hind legs sleepily. The fur at the top of her head was in curlers, and she hadn't even put a tiara on yet. "Have you seen Theodore?"

"I just woke up!" yawned Queen Fifi, ducking into the bathroom and quickly shutting the door. The queen never liked to be seen—even by her own puppies—when she wasn't looking regal!

Passing Rocky and Rollo's bedroom, Rosie heard a loud thump. Pausing, she pressed a silky ear to the door and listened. A strange sawing noise was coming from inside.

Rosie burst into the room. Rocky and Rollo turned around, looking guilty. They each held one end of a two-handled saw and were sawing away at a wooden box.

"What are you two doing?" Rosie asked suspiciously.

"Help!" shouted a quavery voice from inside the wooden box. There was another thump. "Get me out of here!"

"Theodore?" said Rosie. "Is that you?"

"Yes!" cried the butler. "They're trying to cut me in half!"

"What?" gasped Rosie. "Is that true?"

"No," said Rocky.

"Yes," said Rollo.

"Well?" demanded Rosie. "Which one is it?"

"We're *pretending* to saw Theodore in half," said Rocky.

"It's a trick for our magic act," explained Rollo. "Only we're not exactly sure how to do it."

Rosie lifted the wooden box's lid and helped the elderly tortoise crawl out.

"Thank goodness," he gasped, clutching her paw. "That was absolutely terrifying."

"Aw," said Rollo. "It isn't even a real saw, it's just a prop."

"We thought tortoises liked enclosed spaces," said Rocky, shrugging. "You know, like your shell."

"You need to find yourself a new assistant," said Theodore indignantly.

"Maybe you two should do something a little easier," Rosie suggested. "Like card tricks."

"Boring!" scoffed Rocky.

"We're not going to win the talent show with card tricks," said Rollo. "Come on, Rocky. Let's go have breakfast." The princes ran out of the bedroom.

When Theodore had recovered from his fright, Rosie could finally ask him the question she'd been thinking about since she woke up. "Where will Bella Fierce sleep when she visits?"

There were lots of guest rooms in

Pawstone Palace, but Rosie wanted to make sure that Bella's bedroom was perfect for her.

"Perhaps we could put her in the Garden Suite, Your Highness," said Theodore.

"Hmm," said Rosie. The Garden Suite had floral wallpaper, pictures of flowers, and big windows overlooking the garden. "It might be a bit chilly." The palace was very old, and some of the windows were quite drafty.

"What about the King Rufus Bedroom?" Theodore asked.

"Too old-fashioned," said Rosie. Stuffy old antiques didn't seem like Bella Fierce's style.

"Maybe Ms. Fierce might like the Royal Blue Bedroom?" suggested Theodore.

Rosie's eyes lit up. "Her favorite color is blue!" she exclaimed.

Rosie and Theodore walked very, very slowly to the Royal Blue Bedroom. The walls were covered in bright blue silk, and the enormous bed had a matching canopy. "This is perfect!" Rosie said, gazing around. There were a pretty dressing table, a crystal chandelier, a gold clock—

"Oh my goodness!" Rosie gasped. "Look at the time! I was supposed to meet Cleo before my dance lesson!"

Scurrying out of the bedroom, she raced down the stairs and skittered to a halt outside the ballroom. The sound of Bella Fierce singing floated out.

Oh no, she thought. *Did I get the date wrong?* Bella Fierce wasn't supposed to arrive until the day before the show. Opening the door a crack, Rosie peeked inside.

A cat was gracefully twisting and gliding across the dance floor, shaking her lithe, furry body to the beat. But it wasn't Bella Fierce—it was Cleo!

"Way to go!" barked Rosie, clapping her paws.

Embarrassed, Cleo froze.

"Don't stop, Cleo! You're an amazing dancer." Then Rosie had an idea. "You should enter the talent show!"

Cleo shook her head. "I'd love to be in the show, but I'm too shy to dance on stage, all by myself. Unless . . . will you enter the show with me?"

"I'm a terrible dancer," Rosie told her friend. "Just ask Bruno. And besides, I'm too busy planning the show to rehearse an act."

Cleo looked deflated. "That's okay, Rosie," she said. "It's no big deal."

But Rosie could tell it *was* a big deal to her friend. She couldn't let her down. "Don't worry, Cleo! I'll find you a dance partner for the talent show," Rosie promised her.

But where?

Chapter 4

A Dancing Duo

The ballroom door opened, and Priscilla ushered Bruno inside. “Princess Rosie, Bruno is here for your lesson.”

Rosie groaned inwardly, but greeted her teacher politely. “Hi, Bruno.”

Priscilla followed the dance instructor into the ballroom. “Will you be entering the Royal Talent Show?” she asked him.

“Sadly not,” said Bruno, sighing.

"But why?" said Priscilla. "You are such a wonderful dancer."

"That's true," said Bruno, nodding. "I am. But a ballroom dancer needs a partner, and there are no dancers in the kingdom who are truly my equal."

"None at all?" said Priscilla. "Maybe you could take a chance on a dancer you could train . . ." She looked at Bruno hopefully, as if she was hinting at something.

Rosie suddenly had an amazing idea. Bruno needed a dance partner, and Cleo was too scared to dance on her own. They could enter the talent show together. It was perfect!

"Cleo!" she exclaimed.

"What?" said Cleo.

"You can dance with Cleo!" Rosie said.

"That's not what I meant . . ." Priscilla said, her ears drooping with disappointment.

Rosie was so excited by her plan that she didn't hear the sadness in the housekeeper's voice. "Cleo is a really talented dancer," she told Bruno.

"This little kitten?" Bruno said, looking Cleo up and down doubtfully.

"Trust me," said Rosie. "Just watch her and you'll see." Turning to Cleo, she said, "Do the dance routine you were doing when I came in."

"I'm not sure about this," Cleo mewled nervously.

"Don't worry," said Rosie. "It's just me, Bruno, and . . ." She looked around for Priscilla, but the bunny housekeeper had left the room.

Bruno tapped his paw on the floor impatiently. "Well?" he said. "Are you going to dance? I don't have all day."

Rosie turned the Bella Fierce song back on. "Go on," she urged Cleo. "Show him how well you can dance."

At first, Cleo moved stiffly, darting anxious glances at Bruno. Soon, though, Cleo relaxed into the music. Her whole body shimmied and sashayed to the irresistible rhythm of Bella Fierce's song. To finish, Cleo pirouetted on her paws. She spun around so fast her gray fur looked like a blur!

"So . . . ?" said Rosie, eager to hear the dance teacher's verdict. His expression hadn't changed the whole time Cleo had been dancing.

"You lack technique, your tail was droopy, and your paw-work is sloppy," Bruno growled.

Cleo stifled a sad little meow.

But Bruno hadn't finished giving his feedback yet. "But you do have grace, rhythm, and lots of energy."

"That's good, right?" Rosie asked.

"No, it's not good," said Bruno. He leaped up and held out his paws to Cleo. "It's FANTASTIC!" Bruno grabbed Cleo and waltzed her around the ballroom. "You will be the PURRRR-fect partner for me!"

"Yay!" squealed Rosie, her tail wagging excitedly. "Now you can both be in the talent show!"

Rosie's words snapped Bruno back to his usual stern manner. "We have lots of work to do," he told Cleo. "I must teach you to Charleston and cha-cha. You also need to learn to swing dance and do the samba. Are you ready to get started?"

"Okay," said Cleo, looking a bit dazed. "But what about Rosie's dance lesson?"

"Oh yes," said Bruno, his whiskers twitching.

"I've got an idea," said Rosie. She was on

a roll this morning! "Why don't you use my lessons to prepare for the talent show?"

"Hmm," said Bruno, pondering her suggestion. "I'm not sure that Queen Fifi will approve."

"She will!" said Rosie quickly. "She and the king have asked me to organize the talent show, so I'm super busy. I could really use the extra time."

"Are you sure you don't mind?" Cleo asked her.

"Are you kidding?" Rosie said. "Of course I don't mind." *In fact,* she added silently, *I can't think of anything better than skipping my dance lessons!*

"Well then," said Bruno. "It's agreed."

He clapped his paws together briskly. "We'll begin with the fox-trot."

As Bruno and Cleo danced, Rosie wrote a to-do list. There were tickets to sell, programs to make, sets to build, and costumes to design. *How will everything get done in time?* Rosie wondered.

The rest of the morning flew by as Rosie made plans and schedules while Bruno taught Cleo how to rumba.

"Keep your tail straight, but wiggle your hips," Bruno instructed her.

As Bruno counted the beat, Cleo danced forward, her hips moving but her tail staying perfectly still.

"Excellent!" said Bruno. "You look like a wild tiger, not a tame little kitten!"

Rosie heard a growl, but it wasn't a tiger—it was her tummy!

"It's time for lunch," said Bruno. "Dancers need to keep up their energy levels."

As Rosie and Cleo made their way to the dining room, they passed King Charles.

"Have you seen my crown?" the king asked them, scratching his head. "I seem to have misplaced it."

"Sorry, Dad," said Rosie. "I haven't seen it."

"We'll keep an eye out for it, Your Majesty," Cleo promised him.

In the dining room, Priscilla and a group of kitchen maids were clustered around Rocky and Rollo.

"Abracadabra!" cried Rocky, waving his paw over a gold crown.

With a flourish, Rollo pulled a silky purple scarf out of the crown.

"Oooooh!" gasped the maids.

"How did you do that?" Cleo asked the princes.

"Magicians never reveal their secrets," Rocky told her, tapping his nose with his paw.

"Is that Dad's crown?" Rosie said. "He's looking for it, so you'd better give it back."

"No time for an encore," Rollo told the maids. "We've got to go."

"Hey, Cleo," Rocky asked on his way out of the dining room, "do you want to be our new assistant?"

"Sorry, Cleo's already in an act," Rosie informed her brothers. "She's dancing with Bruno."

Priscilla gave a loud sniff.

Oh dear, thought Rosie. *Priscilla's probably feeling left out because she's not in the talent show.* Then she had yet *another* good idea!

"Priscilla," Rosie said, "could you make the costumes for the talent show?"

Priscilla's ears perked up. "Will I get to watch the rehearsals?"

"I guess so," said Rosie.

"Count me in!" said Priscilla, looking much happier.

After lunch, Rosie and Cleo went upstairs to Rosie's bedroom to hang out. Rosie took a book about Bella Fierce off her bookshelf and flipped through it, taking notes. She wanted to be totally prepared for the pop star's visit.

"Did you know that Bella signed her first recording deal when she was still just a kitten?" Rosie asked Cleo. "And that she always drinks tea with honey before performing?"

"No, I didn't know that," said Cleo. "The only thing I know about Bella Fierce is that I love her music." She put on a Bella Fierce song and started to dance around the bedroom.

"I thought you'd be tired after your lesson with Bruno," said Rosie.

"I'm never too tired to dance to Bella Fierce," said Cleo, laughing. "My paws just can't keep still when I listen to her songs."

"Neither can mine," said Rosie, joining in. Cleo taught her the routine she'd done in the ballroom. Soon, Rosie knew all the moves and was happily twisting and twirling along to the music.

"I don't know why you say you're a bad dancer," Cleo panted when they'd stopped dancing and had collapsed on Rosie's bed.

"I guess I only like certain types of

dancing," said Rosie. "Definitely not ballroom dancing."

"Yikes!" said Cleo, checking the time. "I'd better go. Bruno wanted me to practice some more. See you later!"

Lunch break over, Rosie pulled out her to-do list. So far today she'd found a bedroom for Bella Fierce, a dance partner for Cleo, and a job for Priscilla. Tick! Tick! Tick! *Not bad for a morning's work,* thought Rosie. This was going to be the best talent show ever!

Chapter 5

A Very Busy Week

On Monday morning, Rosie popped her head into the ballroom, where Cleo and Bruno were practicing a tango. Priscilla was watching the rehearsal, a rapt look on her face.

"I'm going over to the theater to see how the set is coming along," Rosie told Cleo.

"See you later," Cleo called as Bruno dipped her low.

Outside the palace, a Shetland pony was hitched up to a carriage with Petrovia's royal paw-print crest embossed in gold on its purple doors.

"Can you take me to the theater, please, Chester?" Rosie asked the pony as she climbed into the carriage.

"Sure thing, Your Highness," neighed the pony, bobbing his head respectfully.

Chester started trotting, and the carriage rolled forward.

"Did you know that I won the talent show back when I was just a colt?" Chester said as he clip-clopped toward the theater.

"Really?" said Rosie, intrigued. "What was your act?"

"I tap-danced," said Chester, doing some shuffle ball changes to demonstrate. *TIPPETY-TAP TIPPETY-TAP* went his metal horseshoes as he shuffled his hooves.

"You're still pretty good," said Rosie. "You should enter the show this year."

Chester chuckled. "My dancing days are over, Princess Rosie."

The carriage wheeled up to a grand building with the words ROYAL THEATER carved into the stone facade. Bright, colorful posters advertising the talent show hung outside.

"Oh good," said Rosie. "The posters have gone up." She ticked *Posters* off her list with a feeling of satisfaction.

"I won't be long," she told Chester, jumping down from the carriage.

The red velvet seats inside the theater were empty, but stagehands were working hard to get everything ready for the talent show. A yellow canary was fluttering overhead hanging up lights. A rabbit carpenter with a pencil tucked behind one of his long ears was hammering a piece of scenery, and a dog with paint-splattered fur was decorating a backdrop.

"Princess Rosie!" cried a wrinkly bulldog, hurrying over to greet her. "I'm Max, the stage manager. What an honor!"

"Nice to meet you," Rosie said, shaking

Max's paw. "I just wanted to see how the set was coming along."

"Follow me," said Max, leading Rosie up a short set of stairs onto the stage.

"As you can see," he explained, "the set features the natural beauty of our wonderful kingdom." Wooden backdrops were painted with pretty scenes of Petrovia's rolling hills and green, flower-filled meadows.

"It's lovely," said Rosie, wagging her tail enthusiastically.

SWISH! Her tail hit one of the backdrops. *PLOP!* It toppled over, knocking into another one, and then another. The freshly painted backdrops fell like a row of dominoes!

"I'm so sorry," cried Rosie, staring at the mess she'd just made.

"No harm done," said Max as the stage-hands rushed to pick up the fallen backdrops. Rosie helped them, and soon all the scenery was back in position.

"Keep up the good work," said Rosie, waving good-bye and leaving before she could knock anything else over!

"My paws hurt," moaned Rocky.

"How much farther?" groaned Rollo.

"We're nearly there," Rosie told her brothers.

The princes were helping Rosie carry a

table through the frosty palace grounds on Tuesday morning.

"Set it down here," Rosie said, just inside the main gates. Her brothers let go of the table with sighs of relief.

Rosie spread a white tablecloth on top of the table and hung up a sign that read ROYAL TALENT SHOW TICKETS ON SALE HERE! Her ticket booth was officially open!

"I hope I sell lots of tickets," she said anxiously, looking down at the big stack of tickets. All the money raised by the talent show would go to help sick and needy animals.

"Don't worry," said Rocky. "It will sell

out once everyone hears that Rollo and I are performing again this year."

"Get your tickets for the hottest show in town!" hollered Rollo.

Sure enough, customers started to arrive.

"Two tickets, please," said a squirrel

with glasses perched on her nose. "My son Charlie is doing a juggling act. His dad and I wouldn't miss the show for all the acorns in the world."

"Here you go," said Rosie, handing Charlie's mother her tickets.

Next, Rosie sold a parakeet six tickets. "I'm taking my whole family," he twittered as he paid Rosie for the tickets. "It will be a real tweet—I mean, treat!"

Soon customers crowded around the table. Even with Rocky and Rollo's help, Rosie couldn't keep up with the demand. There were growls of complaint as customers grew impatient, blowing on their paws to stay warm.

"Hey, I was first," grumbled a striped cat.

"Stop pushing," whined a little hamster.

Hamish, who was sprinkling salt on the icy garden paths, called out, "Need a hand, Princess Rosie?"

"Yes, please!" Rosie called back.

"Form a line!" shouted Hamish. "And you'll all be served quickly!"

The customers obediently shuffled into a line. With Hamish helping to keep order, Rosie and her brothers sold tickets as fast as they could.

"Enjoy the show!" Rosie said, handing the very last ticket to a rabbit wearing earmuffs.

The Royal Talent Show was officially sold out!

On Wednesday, Rosie hardly had a chance to catch her breath. First, she helped Theodore polish the talent show trophy. Next, she designed the front cover for the program. Finally, she ordered the refreshments that would be sold during intermission.

"Are there going to be juicy bones?" asked Rocky.

"And doggy choc-o-drops?" asked Rollo.

"Definitely," said Rosie. Those were her favorite treats, too.

She also made sure to order seedy snacks

for the birds and the catnip cookies Cleo loved. She'd barely seen her friend over the past few days, because Cleo and Bruno had been rehearsing their dance nonstop. Rosie couldn't wait to see it!

On Thursday, Rosie and Priscilla went to the ballroom for Cleo and Bruno's costume fitting.

"Ta da!" said Priscilla, unveiling two costumes made from brightly colored feathers.

Priscilla helped Bruno try on his cape and mask.

"SEN-SATIONAL," Bruno said, preening in the mirror.

Rosie helped Cleo put on her towering

headdress. A fountain of feathers shot out of the kitten's head.

"It's, er, very eye-catching," Rosie said. She didn't want to hurt Priscilla's feelings, but the costumes made Cleo and Bruno look like tropical birds!

Cleo and Bruno tried dancing in their costumes. Bruno's mask slipped and covered up his eyes. Cleo's headdress was so heavy she struggled to keep her balance. When Bruno dipped her backward, she toppled over.

"Oh dear," said Rosie. "This isn't working."

"I can fix it," said Priscilla. She got rid of Bruno's mask and adjusted Cleo's headdress, plucking feathers out until it was much shorter.

Cleo and Bruno tried dancing again, and this time their tango went perfectly. As Priscilla watched the dancers, her feet copied Cleo's moves.

"That was great," Rosie said. "You two are performing last, so the show will definitely end with a bang."

"Let's get back to work," Bruno said. "We only have two more days left to rehearse."

Rosie couldn't help yelping with excitement. There were two more days until the show, but only one more day until Bella Fierce arrived!

* * *

"Today is the day, Theodore!" Rosie cried on Friday, running past the butler on her way to the kitchen. "Bella Fierce is coming!"

"Can't say I've ever heard of her," said Theodore. The elderly butler wasn't a fan of pop music.

"She's coming today!" Rosie told Petal as she burst into the kitchen.

Petal didn't need to be told who "she" was. The guinea pig cook was just as excited as Rosie!

"Let's go over the menu one more time, Princess Rosie," Petal said.

"Fish soup for an appetizer," said Rosie.

"Salmon for the main course," said Petal.

"And chocolate pudding for dessert," said Rosie. She had read that Bella Fierce loved chocolate!

"I'd better get started," said Petal, pulling an enormous saucepan out of a cupboard.

Satisfied that dinner preparations were under way, Rosie decided to inspect the Royal Blue Bedroom to make sure it was tidy.

She opened the door and instantly spotted two things that definitely didn't belong in there: Rocky and Rollo!

"Get out of here," Rosie ordered her brothers. "Bella Fierce will be here soon."

"We can't," said Rocky. The princes held

up their paws, revealing that they were chained together!

"What have you done?" Rosie cried, trying not to panic.

"We were practicing our escape trick in here where nobody would see us," said Rollo.

"But we lost the key," said Rocky.

Rosie hunted around the room on her belly, desperately searching for the key. A glint of metal underneath the bed caught her eye. Rosie stretched out a paw and slid the key out, then quickly unlocked her brothers.

"Phew!" said Rocky, untangling himself from the chains.

"That trick still needs a bit of work," admitted Rollo, stretching.

The boys were free—and not a moment too soon. A loud blast of trumpet fanfare came from downstairs. Bella Fierce had arrived!

Chapter 6

Pop Star at the Palace

"I'm coming!" shouted Rosie. She grabbed a tiara from her bedroom and ran down the stairs, her ears flapping. She wanted to make sure she was there to greet Bella. Whoops! Rosie's paw slipped, and she rolled down the last three steps, landing in a heap of curly fur at the bottom of the staircase.

"And this is Princess Rosie," said King Charles.

Queen Fifi, who looked immaculate as usual, did not look impressed by Rosie's dramatic entrance.

"Hi!" said Rosie, shoving her tiara on her head. "I'm your biggest fan, Ms. Fierce."

"That's very sweet of you to say, Princess Rosie," purred Bella Fierce. Her eyes were even more striking in person than in pictures. She lowered them shyly as she bowed to Rosie.

"It's true," said Rocky. "She even sings your songs in the bathtub."

"When she can be bothered to take a bath," said Rollo, giggling.

Rosie glared at Rocky and Rollo. Little brothers could be SO embarrassing!

"As you may have guessed," said King Charles, "these are the princes."

Bella smiled at Rocky and Rollo. Then she winked at Rosie. "I know all about little brothers—I have one, too."

"I know!" said Rosie, remembering something she'd read. "His name is Toby."

"That's right," said Bella, surprised.

"Rosie," said Queen Fifi, "why don't you give Ms. Fierce a tour of the palace before dinner?"

"Should we start with the throne room, Ms. Fierce?" Rosie asked eagerly.

"You can call me Bella, Princess Rosie," said the pop star.

"Only if you call me Rosie," said Rosie, smiling.

"It's a deal," said Bella, smiling back.

Rosie led Bella into the throne room. Banners with purple paw prints on them hung from the ceiling. Two gold thrones with feet shaped like paws stood on a raised platform covered with a canopy of purple silk.

"Oh wow," said Bella. "I can't believe I'm actually at Pawstone Palace."

"I can't believe you're really here, either," said Rosie, laughing.

Bella padded over to the platform and gazed up at the thrones in awe.

"Do you want to sit on one of them?" asked Rosie.

"For real?" said Bella.

"Sure," said Rosie. "Hop on!" Rosie climbed onto King Charles's throne while Bella leaped gracefully onto Queen Fifi's throne and settled herself on the purple velvet cushion.

"All I need now is a tiara," joked Bella.

"Here," said Rosie. "Try this on." She tossed Bella her diamond tiara.

"This is so cool!" said Bella, putting the tiara on her head.

It's funny, Rosie thought. *Bella seems as excited about meeting a princess as I am about meeting a pop star!*

Rosie showed Bella the dining room and the parlor next, and then they went into the drawing room.

"Do you do drawing in here?" Bella asked, puzzled.

"Nope," said Rosie. "It's just a fancy name for a living room."

A bunny maid hopped up to Bella, holding an album. "Excuse me, Ms. Fierce," she said. "Can I please have your autograph?"

"Of course," Bella said graciously, signing her name.

Soon, a whole crowd of maids had gathered around Bella to get her signature!

When Bella had finished signing autographs, Rosie continued the tour. They peeped into the ballroom, where Cleo and Bruno were practicing their dance.

"That's Cleo, my best friend," said Rosie. "She's rehearsing for the talent show."

"They look really good," said Bella. "I can't wait to see all the acts tomorrow."

Rosie suddenly realized something. "I haven't shown you where you're going to sleep!"

She led Bella upstairs. "This is the Haunted Tower," said Rosie, passing the entrance to one of the castle's many towers.

Bella shivered. "Is it really haunted?"

Rosie laughed. "People say it's haunted by the ghost of King Grizzlebone III, but that's just a silly story." She and Cleo had once gone up to the top of the tower late at night on a dare. They hadn't found a ghost—just King Charles having a midnight snack!

Finally, Rosie and Bella arrived at the Royal Blue Bedroom. "This is where you'll stay," Rosie said, flinging the door open.

Bella padded in and looked around the room.

"It's gorgeous," she purred happily. "Blue is my—"

"Favorite color!" Rosie finished Bella's sentence for her.

Leaving Bella to unpack, Rosie got ready for dinner. She brushed her fur, put on a pretty sapphire-studded collar, and went downstairs.

"What's she like?" Cleo asked, rushing over to Rosie. "Is she fierce like her name?"

"She's not fierce at all," said Rosie. "She's really nice."

Rosie and Cleo made their way into the dining room, which Theodore had set with the palace's best china and silver.

King Charles and Queen Fifi sat at either end of the long wooden dining table. Rosie and Cleo were on either side of Bella, with the princes opposite them.

"This is delicious," said Bella, tasting Petal's fish soup.

Petal beamed proudly and ladled another helping into Bella's bowl.

"Your dance looked great," Bella told Cleo when they had moved on to the salmon main course.

"Thanks," said Cleo. "I'm feeling really nervous about doing it in front of an audience."

"Can I tell you a secret?" Bella whispered.

Rosie and Cleo nodded.

"I get stage fright every time I perform," Bella confided.

"Really?" said Cleo. "But you seem so cool and confident."

"Bella Fierce isn't my real name," Bella

said. "I'm really Bella Smith, but I created a bold, fearless character called Bella Fierce to help me onstage. Maybe you should do the same, Cleo."

"That's a great idea," exclaimed Rosie.

"It might work," said Cleo. She playfully swiped her paw at Bella and growled. "Call me Cleo Savage!"

"We're in the talent show, too," Rocky told Bella.

"What type of act are you doing?" asked Bella.

"A magic show," said Rollo. "Want to see one of our tricks?"

"Sure," said Bella.

"We can make this dessert float in the air," announced Rocky, picking up a huge crystal bowl full of chocolate pudding.

"I'm not sure that's a good idea . . ." said Rosie, but her brothers ignored her.

Pointing his fork like a wand, Rollo commanded, "Chockity rockity boo! Make this pudding float!"

"Hey presto!" shouted Rocky, letting go of the crystal bowl. *CRASH!* The bowl fell onto the dining table. *SPLASH!* Chocolate pudding flew everywhere, including all over Bella Fierce's face!

"Oops!" said Rocky. "That wasn't supposed to happen."

"Go to your room!" Queen Fifi ordered

the princes, who slunk off with their tails between their legs.

"I'm so sorry," King Charles apologized to Bella. "The princes are such rascals."

"It was actually pretty funny," Bella said, chuckling as she licked chocolate off her paws. "And this pudding is so yummy!" Luckily, Petal had more pudding in the kitchen, so everyone—except for Rocky and Rollo—could still have dessert.

After dinner, Rosie said, "There's a room I want you to see." She and Cleo took Bella into the music room, which had a grand piano and many other musical instruments.

"What a beautiful piano," Bella said, gently running her paws over the ivory keys.

"Will you play us something?" Cleo asked shyly.

"I'll play you my new song," said Bella. "But you've got to do something for me in return."

"What's that?" Rosie asked.

"Dance along!" said Bella, tucking her tail underneath her and sitting down at the piano.

"Today's gonna be a big success," sang Bella. *"Yeah, I feel like a real princess."*

Rosie and Cleo danced around the room to the uplifting pop tune.

"What do you think?" Bella asked them when she'd finished playing.

"I loved it!" Rosie cried.

"Good," said Bella, smiling. "Because you inspired me to write it!"

"Bathtime," said Queen Fifi, entering the music room.

"Aw!" said Rosie. "We were having so much fun."

"You need to get that chocolate pudding off your whiskers," said Queen Fifi, ruffling Rosie's fur. "Tomorrow's a big day, so you must look your best."

Rosie wagged her tail and let out a yip of excitement. Only one more sleep until the Royal Talent Show!

The Talent Show

"Time to go!" Rosie cried, knocking on her brothers' bedroom door. The day of the Royal Talent Show had finally arrived, and it was nearly time to leave for the theater.

When nobody answered, Rosie opened the door and saw her brothers standing in front of a mirror.

"What an honor," said Rocky. "We are deeply humbled."

"We'd like to thank our parents, and of course all the citizens of Petrovia," said Rocky, dabbing his eyes with his paw.

"Um, what are you doing?" Rosie asked them.

"We're practicing for when we win the talent show," Rocky informed her.

"So we sound surprised," Rollo added.

Thinking back to the previous evening's chocolate pudding disaster, Rosie knew she wouldn't have to pretend to be surprised if her brothers won. "Don't get your hopes up," she warned them.

Next, Rosie knocked gently on the Royal Blue Bedroom's door.

"Come in," called Bella.

"Did you sleep well?" Rosie asked Bella, who was sitting at her dressing table, brushing her fur.

"Like a kitten," Bella purred. "The bed was really comfy."

"Are you ready to go?" said Rosie.

"Nearly," said Bella, putting on a cool black collar with punky metal spikes. "I just have to make sure I look like a pop star." She winked her blue eye at Rosie. "What do you think?"

"You definitely look like Bella Fierce now," Rosie said, winking back.

Next, Rosie went into the ballroom. "We've got to go now," Rosie told Cleo and Bruno, who were having one last practice.

"I've got your costumes," said Priscilla, holding up the two feathered outfits.

Everyone gathered outside the palace in the cold air. The sound of jingling bells rang out across the snowy grounds. Chester trotted up the drive, pulling a big, shiny red sleigh.

"I thought we'd take the royal sleigh, as it snowed again last night," said Chester.

"Wonderful idea," said King Charles, climbing into the sleigh.

The rest of the royal family, followed by Bella, Cleo, Bruno, and Priscilla, climbed into the sleigh and snuggled under warm blankets. Animals waved and cheered as the royal sleigh glided smoothly over the snow to the theater.

"Thank you! Thank you!" said Bruno, waving back grandly.

"I think they were waving to the king and queen," Cleo whispered in Rosie's ear.

"Bruno thinks he *is* king," said Rosie, giggling. "King of the dance floor, that is!"

"We're here!" announced Chester, coming to a stop. Everyone piled out of the sleigh and went inside the theater.

"Wow!" said Cleo, gazing at the stage in awe.

Rosie beamed. The set *did* look amazing!

As King Charles, Queen Fifi, and Bella took their seats in the royal box, everyone else went backstage to get ready for the show. Rosie rushed around with a clipboard checking that all the acts had arrived and had everything they needed.

"How are you feeling?" Rosie asked Cleo, who was pacing nervously.

"Great!" barked Bruno, answering for his partner. "I just LOVE being onstage."

"I'm a little nervous," Cleo admitted. She and Rosie peeped out from behind the thick red velvet stage curtains. There wasn't an empty seat in the auditorium. The audience chattered excitedly, waiting for the show to start. Cleo gulped. "Now I'm a lot nervous."

"Just remember, you're Cleo Savage," Rosie told her friend. "You'll be amazing."

Max, the stage manager, hurried over to Rosie. "One minute to curtain up, Princess Rosie!"

Rosie's heart pounded with excitement. This was it! The Royal Talent Show was about to begin!

There was a deafening cheer as King Charles stood and thanked the audience for coming. "And now, on with the show!" the king said.

The curtain rose, and a spotlight shone on a group of baby mice in tutus.

"Awww," cooed the audience as the tiny

white mice tottered on their little pink feet performing an adorable ballet dance.

"Charlie, you're on," whispered Rosie when the mice had finished. She handed her squirrel friend his acorns.

Watching from the wings, Rosie held her breath and hoped that Charlie wouldn't drop any of his nuts as he tossed them higher and higher in the air. For his grand finale, Charlie spun around and balanced all three acorns on the tip of his fluffy tail!

"That was brilliant," Rosie said as Charlie scampered offstage.

A rabbit ventriloquist performed, followed by a hula-hooping cat and the cheerleading maids. Then it was Petal's turn. The theater's chandeliers rattled and all of the dogs in the audience whimpered as the guinea pig cook strained to reach the high notes.

The audience oohed and aahed at a daredevil dog's fire-eating act and chuckled as two cats named Fizzy and Dizzy clowned around, squirting each other with water.

Next, the Twittertown Choir fluttered onto the stage. Flying in formation, they chirped a medley of songs from popular musicals. "Bravo!" cried the audience, giving the choir a standing ovation. It would be a tough act to follow, but Rocky and Rollo weren't daunted.

"Prepare to be amazed," Rocky told Rosie and Cleo.

"Good luck," Rosie said. From what she'd seen, they would need it!

Rocky and Rollo's act started well. They did a few card tricks, and then Rocky pulled scarves out of Rollo's crown.

So far, so good, thought Rosie.

Rollo wheeled a wooden cabinet decorated with dragons and magical symbols onto the stage.

"For our next trick," said Rocky, "we'll need a volunteer."

"Me!" cried Bruno, rushing out from the side of the stage. "I'll do it!"

"Excellent," said Rollo, opening the cabinet's door. "Step right in here, sir."

Enjoying the attention, Bruno waved at the audience as he stepped inside the cabinet.

"We will now make him disappear," said Rocky.

The puppy princes pointed their wands at the cabinet and chanted:

"Abracadabra, alacazeer,

Make this doggy disappear!"

Rocky flung open the cabinet's door. The audience gasped. Bruno had vanished!

"We will now bring him back," said Rollo.

Once again, the princes pointed their wands at the cabinet and cried:

"Abracadabra, alacazeer,

Make this doggy reappear!"

With a flourish, Rollo opened the door, revealing . . . an empty cabinet!

Rocky and Rollo exchanged worried looks.

"Let's try that again," said Rocky.

The princes shouted the magic words again, but the cabinet remained empty. Faint thumps and muffled yelps were coming from inside it.

The audience began to murmur and shift restlessly in their seats.

Uh-oh, thought Rosie.

"We need to get them off!" she told Max.

The stage manager dimmed the lights, and Rosie helped Rocky and Rollo wheel the cabinet offstage.

Thinking fast, Rosie handed Hamish his bagpipes. "You're on!"

As Hamish went onstage and started playing a lively jig on his bagpipes, Rosie tried to free Bruno from the cabinet.

"Let me out!" the dance teacher demanded furiously. "It's time for my tango!"

Rosie tried with all her might, but she couldn't break Bruno out of the cabinet.

"I'll get help," she promised him, running to find Max.

"The carpenters can get him out," the stage manager told her, calling for help on his walkie-talkie. "But it could take a while."

Rosie didn't have any time to spare! Bruno and Cleo were the only act left to perform, and Hamish had nearly finished his tune.

"What are we going to do?" Cleo asked Rosie.

"You'll have to dance on your own," Rosie said.

Cleo's eyes widened in alarm. "I can't!"

"Please," begged Rosie. "You're an amazing dancer, and the show really needs a fantastic closing act."

"I'll do it," Cleo said. "But only on one condition."

"Anything," said Rosie.

"You dance with me!" said Cleo.

Chapter 8

The Show Must Go On

"But I'm a terrible dancer," said Rosie.

"No you're not," said Cleo. "We'll dance to a Bella Fierce song."

Rosie hesitated, remembering how hard Cleo had practiced for this moment. She didn't want to let her best friend down. She also didn't want to disappoint the audience, who were expecting one more act.

"Okay," said Rosie. "Let's do it." She put

on Bruno's feathered cape and mask. *Hopefully nobody will recognize me if I make a fool of myself,* Rosie thought.

"There's been a last-minute change of music," Rosie told Max. "The next act will perform to Bella Fierce's 'Wild, Not Mild.'"

"I'll let the sound engineer know," Max said, taking out his walkie-talkie again.

Giving one last blast on his bagpipes, Hamish left the stage to enthusiastic applause.

"Ready to be Cleo Savage?" Rosie asked.

"Ready as I'll ever be!" Cleo said.

Rosie and Cleo strutted onto the stage and struck feisty poses. Rosie blinked, adjusting to the glare of the spotlight. Luckily, it was bright, so she couldn't see the audience. She could pretend that they were alone in her bedroom, dancing just for fun.

The first strains of Bella's hit song sounded and Rosie and Cleo began to dance. They grooved and glided across the stage, kicking their paws and shaking their tails in time to the beat. The song was about going wild, and that's exactly what Rosie did. She threw herself into the funky music, using every ounce of energy she had.

The dance routine finished with Rosie holding Cleo's front paws and spinning her around and around. Cleo's back paws lifted off the ground as Rosie twirled faster and faster.

"Woo-hoo!" cheered the crowd.

When the song ended, Rosie and Cleo took a bow, and the audience gave them a standing ovation. Squinting, Rosie peered up at the royal box. Her parents and Bella were on their feet, too!

Backstage, Rosie squealed, "We did it!"

"Thank you so much for dancing with me!" said Cleo. "You were amazing!"

"So were you!" said Rosie, hugging her friend.

"Well done to all the contestants," King Charles said, walking onto the stage with Queen Fifi. "All the acts have performed, so it's time—"

"Wait!" howled Bruno. He ran onto the

stage, finally out of the cabinet. "There's one more act! I haven't danced yet." He looked around wildly. "Where's my partner?"

"I'll dance with you!" cried a voice. Priscilla hopped onto the stage. "I've been watching the rehearsals—I know all the steps!"

Before Bruno could reply, King Charles said, "Excellent! What a lovely surprise!"

Tango music began to play. Bruno took Priscilla's paws and led her around the stage, whisker to whisker. Priscilla danced gracefully to the music, her elegant movements perfectly in sync with Bruno's. It was hard to believe that they had never danced together before.

"Priscilla's really good!" said Cleo, watching the dancers from the side of the stage.

The housekeeper looked happier than Rosie had ever seen her before. "I can't believe I didn't realize that Priscilla really wanted to dance," Rosie said, suddenly understanding why Priscilla had been so interested in the rehearsals.

For their dramatic finale, Bruno dipped Priscilla so low that her long ears grazed the floor.

"Yay!" cheered Rosie along with the rest of the audience.

"Now I think we are finally ready to announce the winner," said King Charles. He chuckled. "Unless we have any other last-minute surprises?" He paused for a moment and then continued, "Ladies and gentlemen, please welcome this year's judge, singing sensation Bella Fierce!"

The audience whooped and hollered as Bella padded onto the stage, looking every inch the superstar she was.

"I really enjoyed watching all the acts! It has been very hard to make a decision," Bella said. "But the winner of this year's Royal Talent Show is . . . the Twittertown Choir."

"They were great," said Rosie, hoping Cleo wouldn't be upset.

Cleo nodded. "They really deserved to win," she said sweetly.

The choir chirped with delight as they flew onto the stage to collect their prize.

"Congratulations to you all," said Queen Fifi, handing the leader of the choir a trophy. Shiny and gold, it had a royal paw print on the top.

The audience applauded until King Charles held up a paw for silence. "Ms. Fierce," he addressed Bella. "We'd all love to hear *you* sing. Will you do us the honor?"

"Well . . ." said Bella. "I have been working on a new song. Would you like to hear it?"

The audience let out a roar.

"I'll take that as a yes," said Bella, laughing. "But I'll need some backup dancers.

Would the two dancers who performed to my song be willing to help me out?"

Rosie and Cleo exchanged looks. "Does she mean us?" Cleo asked.

"I think so!" Rosie replied.

They ran back onto the stage, and the audience cheered.

"I'd like to dedicate this song to my new friend, Rosie," Bella told the crowd. She launched into her song about feeling like a princess.

Rosie and Cleo danced joyfully, waving their paws and wiggling their tails. The audience clapped along, and everyone joined in with the chorus: *"Today's gonna be a big success. Yeah, I feel like a real princess."*

When the song was over, Rosie and Cleo took a bow with Bella.

"Thanks, girls," said Bella. "I really do feel like a princess today."

"And I feel like a pop star," said Rosie, grinning.

After the show, they all went backstage. The other performers crowded around Bella to shake her paw and get her autograph.

"I can't believe we lost again," sulked Rollo.

"Cheer up," Rosie told her brothers. "There's always next year."

"The contest was rigged," grumbled Rocky.

"Well, you did trap Bruno inside a cabinet," Rosie said.

"I thought you'd be happy about that," said Rollo. "No more dance lessons!"

"Did someone mention dance lessons?" said Bruno, coming over. "You were surprisingly good, Princess Rosie. I have obviously been teaching you well."

"Er, thanks," said Rosie.

Turning to Cleo, Bruno said, "I hope you don't mind, but I've asked Priscilla to be my dance partner from now on."

"That's fine," said Cleo. "You two are perfect partners."

"And so are we," said Rosie, putting a paw around Cleo.

“I agree,” said Queen Fifi, joining them.

“You’re not angry that I danced in the show?” Rosie asked her mother nervously. She was worried that dancing to pop music wasn’t a very princessy thing to do.

“Of course not,” said Queen Fifi. “I’m delighted to see you enjoying dancing at last.”

“You did what it took to save the Royal Talent Show,” said King Charles. “I’d expect nothing less from the future queen of Petrovia.”

“We are so proud of you,” said Queen Fifi. “Because of all your hard work, the show was a huge success and raised lots of money for animals in need.”

Rosie glowed with pride. She was so happy to have helped her parents—as well as the less fortunate animals of Petrovia.

"I should be going," said Bella, who had finished greeting her fans.

"Thank you so much for coming," said Queen Fifi.

"The pleasure was all mine," said Bella. She curtsied politely to the king and queen, but hugged Cleo and Rosie.

"I'm going on a world tour soon," said Bella. "How would you two like to be my dancers?"

Rosie looked at Cleo and then shook her head. "No, thanks," she said. "I'm sure it would be really fun, but my place is here in Petrovia."

"And my place is with Rosie," said Cleo.

Rosie wagged her tail happily. Being a pop star had been fun, but being a puppy princess was even better!

Read on for more Puppy Princess fun!

Puppy Princess #4

Flower Girl Power

"Dotty!" barked Rosie, her tail wagging wildly. She ran to her cousin and they nuzzled each other's noses affectionately.

"It's so good to see you, Rosie," said Dotty, who had fluffy hair like her mother and spots like her father. "There's someone I'd like you to meet." She beckoned to a handsome brown-and-white terrier. "This is my friend Jack Russell."

"Nice to meet you, Princess Rosie," said Jack, bowing to her. "Dotty has told me so much about you."

"What's she told you about us?" Rocky asked impishly.

"She told me that you two are royal terrors," teased Jack. "And that you love to play ball. Want to play catch in the garden?"

"Yippee!" Rocky and Rollo cried together. Yelping with excitement, the puppy princes ran off with Jack.

"Jack seems really nice," said Rosie.

"Yes, he is," said Dotty. "He's very special."

A bell tinkled inside the palace.

"We'd better not be late for tea," said Dotty.

Rosie and Dotty joined their parents in an elegant parlor. There were lace doilies on every surface, and on the table was a fancy china tea set. King Charles was eyeing a silver platter of cookies greedily.

"We're here!" cried Rocky, bursting into the room. Rollo tumbled in after his brother, panting noisily before grabbing a cookie.

"Oh no!" gasped Duchess Coco, horrified. "Look at the carpet!"

The princes had tracked muddy paw prints all over the rug!

"I'll get that cleaned up," said Jack. He quickly brushed away the dirt. "The princes just didn't want to be late," he explained.

"Thanks, Jack," said Dotty.

"Did you boys have fun?" King Charles asked, helping himself to several cookies.

"It was great," said Rollo, spraying crumbs everywhere.

"Visiting here isn't going to be totally boring for once," said Rocky through a mouthful of cookie.

Duchess Coco spluttered on her tea.

"I'm sure the boys don't mean that," Queen Fifi interjected hastily.

"Sorry," said Rocky. "I just meant that Jack is awesome."

"We think so, too," said the duke.

"Actually," said Duchess Coco, "Dotty and Jack have some news . . ."

Jack went to sit by Dotty, putting one of his paws on top of hers. Dotty looked up at him adoringly.

Rosie suddenly remembered the bridal magazine, the photograph on Dotty's bedside table, and what her cousin had said about dancing at a wedding. Everything suddenly fell into place. How had she not figured it out earlier? "You're getting married!" she blurted out.

Duchess Coco looked annoyed that Rosie had interrupted her big announcement, but Dotty and Jack nodded happily.

"Congratulations!" shouted Rosie, hugging her cousin.

Rocky and Rollo gave Jack high fives with their paws.

"When is the wedding going to be?" asked Queen Fifi.

"Soon, hopefully," said Dotty. "Once we've chosen somewhere to have it."

"Not too soon. I need to learn how to dance first," joked Jack.

"Why don't you get married at Pawstone Palace?" offered King Charles.

"Really?" asked Dotty.

"Of course," said Queen Fifi. "We'd be honored to host our niece's wedding."

"That's so kind of you," said Jack.

"Actually, we have another favor to ask," said Dotty. Turning to her cousin, she popped the question. "Rosie, would you be my bridesmaid?"

"Yes!" Rosie barked happily.